For Holly: Merry Christmas always.
—L.R.

When Santa Lost His Ho! Ho! Ho!
Copyright © 2008 by Laura Rader

Manufactured in China.
All rights reserved. No part of this book may be used or reproduced in any manner whatsoever without written
permission except in the case of brief quotations embodied in critical articles and reviews. For information address HarperCollins
Children's Books, a division of HarperCollins Publishers, 1350 Avenue of the Americas, New York, NY 10019.
www.harpercollinschildrens.com

Library of Congress Cataloging-in-Publication Data is available.
ISBN 978-0-06-114139-3 (trade bdg.) — ISBN 978-0-06-114140-9 (lib. bdg.)

Typography by Rachel Zegar
1 2 3 4 5 6 7 8 9 10
❖
First Edition

When Santa Lost His HO! HO! HO!

Laura Rader

HarperCollinsPublishers

Christmas was just a few days away. The North Pole was buzzing with activity. The reindeer were practicing their takeoff. And the elves were putting finishing touches on the toys—with lots of help from Mrs. Claus.

Santa looked tired.
"We need a little break," he said.
"How about a song and dance to
get us going?" asked Mrs. Claus.

Music and laughter
rocked the workshop.
But something wasn't right.
Something was missing.
Santa was quiet.

"What is it, dear?" asked Mrs. Claus.
"Have you lost something, sir?" asked an elf.
Santa scratched his head.
He cleared his throat.
"You could say that," he said.

"What is it?" asked the elves. "We'll help you find it!"
Everyone waited for Santa's answer.
"I think that I've lost my laugh!" he said.
Everyone gasped. Oh no!
Santa had lost his HO! HO! HO!

This was serious!
How could there be Christmas without Santa's HO! HO! HO!

Santa tried some home remedies.
They didn't work.

He went to see Dr. Giddy.
The doctor prescribed funny movies
and a large dose of jokes.

Everyone was eager to help.

But the best Santa
could manage was a
little "ha ha,"
a weak "yippee," and
a faint "yee ha?"
But no HO! HO! HO!

The local paper broke the news.
Reporters and photographers gathered
outside Santa's workshop.

This story was **big!**

Around the world, people heard the news.

Back at the North Pole, the elves and Mrs. Claus
kept trying to help Santa HO! HO! HO!

Nothing worked.

The reindeer even offered
a surefire remedy—cocoa!
Santa enjoyed it, but his laugh
was a no-show.

goo!

Santa decided to check his mail.
He *always* read every single letter himself.
But he'd been so busy trying to HO! HO! HO!
that the mail had really piled up!

Mrs. Claus noticed that Santa looked tired—
even a bit cranky.
"Mr. Claus," she said, "please take a nap.
We'll organize your mail. Now scoot!"
"Well . . . maybe just a few winks," Santa said.

Santa settled in for a short winter's nap.

Mrs. Claus and the elves got busy.
They opened the mail.

They sorted it and put it into neat stacks.
"Look at all these wonderful letters!"
said Mrs. Claus.
There were also some unusual gifts.

Mrs. Claus held up a drawing from a girl named Holly.
"Look at this one!" she exclaimed.
The elves and Mrs. Claus laughed until they cried.
"I have an idea!" said Mrs. Claus. "Gather the letters
and follow me to the workshop!"

"We'll have lots of room up here!" Mrs. Claus told the elves.
"But *hurry*! Santa will be awake soon!"

Santa awoke from his nap feeling much better.
But there was still no sign of his HO! HO! HO!
He heard giggles coming from the kitchen.
"Sounds like everyone is having fun!" said Santa.
"I'll join you after I read some letters."

"Your mail is in the workshop, dear,"
said Mrs. Claus.
"So you can sit in your favorite chair
when you read," said the postmaster elf.
"Great idea!" said Santa.

Santa headed for the workshop.
The elves and Mrs. Claus waited by the kitchen window—
to watch *and* to listen.
One minute passed.
Then two.
It was so quiet, you could hear a snowflake fall.

"I don't hear a thing." Mrs. Claus tsked.
"It's not working!" moaned the postmaster elf.

Then there came . . .
a faint rumble . . .
a distant chuckle . . .
and finally . . .
a mighty, booming,
very familiar, and
oh! so jolly . . .

Santa's HO! HO! HO! was back!

The reporters and photographers heard it. Folks in town heard it. *Everyone, everywhere around the world, heard it!*

Mrs. Claus jumped for joy. The elves shouted with glee. The reindeer pranced and danced.

HO! HO!

HO! HO! HO!

Santa thanked everyone for their pictures—especially Holly! He promised that this would be the merriest, jolliest Christmas EVER. And it was.

"Bad day" drawing by Holly makes Santa jolly!